| | | |
|---|---|---|
| | *Introduction* | 4 |
| | *The People in This Story* | 5 |
| 1 | You Must Have a Dream | 7 |
| 2 | 'Help! Help!' | 8 |
| 3 | The News on TV | 12 |
| 4 | Mike Murray | 17 |
| 5 | A Very Exciting Day | 21 |
| 6 | Lunch on Granville Island | 26 |
| 7 | A New Friend? | 31 |
| 8 | Flowers for Mei | 36 |
| 9 | Jack Pearson | 42 |
| 10 | An Invitation | 46 |
| 11 | The Man in the Silver Car | 51 |
| 12 | Loi's Story | 56 |
| | *Points for Understanding* | 61 |

# Introduction

Dreams come to you when you are asleep. Thoughts, ideas and pictures come into your mind. Dreams can be happy, or dreams can be sad. But you can also dream when you are awake. These dreams are your hopes and wishes for the future. This is the story of a young girl's dream and how it came true.

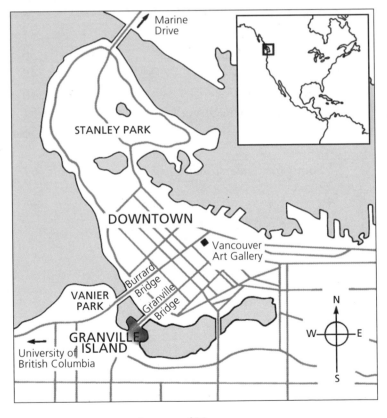

*A map of Vancouver*

# The People in This Story

**Mei Nguyen**
is 18 years old. She was born in
Hanoi, in Vietnam.
She now lives in Canada, in
the city of Vancouver.

**Lan Thi**
is Mei's grandmother. She
brought Mei to Canada
eight years ago.

**Alfredo Santini**
has a shoe store in Vancouver.
Mei works for him.

**Mike Murray**
works for a television
company.

**Sandy McLaren**
is Mei's new friend.

**Mr X**
is a mysterious man in a big silver car. He will change the lives
of the people in the story.

# 1

## You Must Have a Dream

You must always have a dream. Life can be difficult and a dream helps you when life is hard. A dream gives you hope. My dream is this – I love to run and I want to win a gold medal in the Olympic Games.

I know that I'm a good runner. I'm very fast and one day, perhaps I will run in the Olympic Games. My dream will come true. I believe in it.

My grandmother and I live in Vancouver, in western Canada. Vancouver is a beautiful city on the Pacific Ocean. Every evening after work, I run along the sea front near Vanier Park. I love to see the colours on the water as the sun goes down. I run past men with fishing rods in their hands. Sometimes they catch a fish but most of the time they sit in silence. I run past young people. They hold hands and look at the sunset. They have their dreams. But my dream is different.

Nine years ago my mother died. My grandmother and I left Hanoi in Vietnam and we came to Canada. I was ten years old. My grandmother and I are alone in the world. There are no other people in my family. My father died when I was a baby. He was killed in the war. I don't remember him at all. But I have many good memories of my mother. She was a wonderful woman. I loved her very much. She worked hard. She was clever, brave and strong. I want to be strong and brave, too.

Things were not easy when we first came to Canada. Everything was so different from Vietnam. I had to learn to speak English. I had to study hard. I wanted my grandmother to be proud of me.

In my last year at school, my teacher said, 'Mei, do you want to go to university?'

'Yes,' I said, 'but – but it's impossible. I have to get a job. I have to earn money to help my grandmother.'

So now I work in Mr Alfredo Santini's shoe store. But things will change.

Before she died, my mother said to me, 'Mei, live your life fully. Be happy! Be brave! Be successful!'

I will try to be all of these things.


# 2

## 'Help! Help!'


*Sunday*

Today was Sunday, so I didn't have to go to work. I stayed at home in the morning and helped my grandmother with the housework. In the afternoon, I went running as usual. There are lots of good places to run in Vancouver. Today, I decided to go somewhere different. I went to Stanley Park to run along the old sea wall.

It was a fine day but there was a cold wind. There were not many people in the area. At this time of the year, the geese are getting ready to fly south to warmer countries. I stopped to watch a flock of those big beautiful birds. They flew low over the water. Near me, there was a fair-haired woman with her little boy.

'Look, Tom! Look at the birds!' she shouted to him. But Tom didn't listen. He picked up some small stones and he ran to the edge of the sea wall. He threw the stones into the water. Then suddenly his foot slipped and he fell. Down he went – *splash* – into the cold, grey water.

'Mommy!' the boy cried. 'Mommy!'

'Help! Help!' his mother shouted. 'My boy! My boy! Help! I can't swim!'

I ran to the edge of the sea wall and I jumped into the cold, grey sea. I caught the little boy in my arms. Two young men put out their arms. They helped us out of the water, first Tom and then me.

'Oh, my darling, my darling!' Tom's mother cried. 'You're safe. Thank God!' There were tears in her eyes and her hands shook.

One of the young men took off his jacket and covered the little boy with it.

'Come on,' he said. 'I have my car near here. We have to get that boy to hospital right away.'

'Yes, of course, yes,' Tom's mother said. She looked at me. Tears ran down her cheeks.

'You saved my boy. What can I say? You were so brave,' she said.

'Come on! Hurry up,' said the young man with the car. 'Let's go.' They got into the car.

'I also have a car,' the other young man said to me. 'Can I give you a ride? You're very wet and it's cold.'

*Down he went – splash – into the cold, grey water.*

'No, it's all right,' I answered. 'I live near here.'

This wasn't true but I didn't want to ride in a car with a strange man. I didn't stay any more. I was cold and I wanted to be at home. I ran all the way home to try to get warm.

———

When I got home, the apartment was dark and silent. My grandmother was asleep.

'That's good,' I thought. 'I won't tell Grandma what happened. She worries about everything.'

I quickly took off my wet clothes and had a hot shower. I put my track suit in the washing-machine.

My grandmother usually does all the cooking for us, but I decided to prepare supper as a surprise. I wanted to make her favourite Vietnamese dish of vegetables and rice. I started to cut up some vegetables. A few minutes later, my grandmother came into the kitchen.

'Mei, I didn't hear you come in,' she said.

I smiled but didn't say anything.

My grandmother looked at me. Then she said, 'Is it raining?'

'No,' I answered. 'It's cold and windy, but it isn't raining.'

'Then why did you wash your hair again?' my grandmother asked me. 'You washed it last night.'

My grandmother notices everything. It's quite difficult to have secrets from her.

'Grandma,' I said. 'I rescued a boy from the sea. That's why my hair is wet. He was only a small boy. He slipped off the wall and fell into the sea.'

My grandmother put her arms around me.

'You're a brave girl, Mei,' she said. 'I was proud of your mother. And I'm proud of you.'

Then she took a knife and began to cut the vegetables into smaller pieces.

'You jumped into the cold sea in this weather?' she went on. 'You silly girl. You will probably catch a cold.'

# 3

# The News on TV

*Monday*

My grandmother's words came true. I have a bad cold. I woke up this morning with a sore throat. My head ached, my skin was hot, I had a temperature. I wasn't well. But I didn't want to stay in bed. I got dressed and had breakfast quickly.

'Why are you in a hurry?' asked my grandmother.

'Grandma, it's a busy time at the store,' I said. 'I have to put out the winter boots and shoes. I have to put them in the shop window.'

'Your eyes are red. I think that you have a temperature. Would you like some medicine?'

'No, thank you. Believe me, Grandma, I'm fine,' I said.

'Well,' she answered. 'It's your decision.'

I left the apartment and went to work. But at about

eleven o'clock, I could not work any more.

'What's the matter?' asked Mr Santini.

'I'm not well,' I said.

Mr Santini put his hand on my forehead.

'My goodness, Mei! Your skin is hot! You have a high temperature,' he said. 'You must go home immediately!'

'But —' I said.

'No! Listen to me,' Mr Santini said. 'I'm going to call a taxi for you right now. Go home and stay in bed.'

'But Mr Santini, the winter shoes – the window —'

'They can wait, Mei. Your health is more important. Shall I call your grandmother and tell her?' Mr Santini asked.

'No, no, please! And please don't call a taxi,' I said. 'I can't pay for a taxi.'

'Nonsense, girl! Santini's Shoe Store will pay for the taxi,' Mr Santini said. 'Go home. Get into bed and stay there!'

I went home and got into bed. I didn't want to do anything else. My grandmother made me a hot drink and I took some medicine.

I slept most of the day. But every time I woke up, I saw my grandmother. She was sitting on an old chair next to my bed.

———

At about six o'clock in the evening, I woke up again. This time I knew that I was better. I was hungry. Wonderful smells came to my room from the kitchen.

'Grandma!' I called. She came immediately.

'How are you?' she asked.

'I'm much better and I'm very hungry.'

'I'll bring you your supper,' my grandmother said. 'It's almost ready.'

We ate our meal, then we watched the news on TV. Suddenly I saw a young fair-haired woman. It was Tom's mother!

A reporter asked her a question and she answered, 'My name is Valerie Manning. Yesterday afternoon, my son,

Tom, fell into the sea at Stanley Park. I panicked. But luckily a young Asian woman heard my shouts. She jumped into the sea. She saved my boy's life. Everything happened so quickly. A man took me and my son to the hospital. And the girl disappeared. She was really great. She saved my boy's life. My son Tom is fine now. He and I and Tom's father want to thank this wonderful girl. Please young lady, if you or your family are watching this programme, call the TV studio. Please tell the studio your telephone number.'

I quickly turned off the television. There was a moment of silence.

'Mei,' said my grandmother, 'why did you turn the TV off? Was that —?'

'Yes,' I said. 'That was the little boy's mother.'

'What are you going to do?' my grandmother asked me.

'I don't want to do anything,' I said. 'The woman said thank you. That's enough.'

'Mei, you must decide. But I think you have to call the TV studio,' my grandmother said. 'Mrs Manning wants to speak to you. You saved her son's life.'

'I know, Grandma,' I said. 'But —'

'Call the studio,' my grandmother replied.

'Can we finish our supper first?' I asked.

'Of course, my little one,' my grandmother said. She always calls me 'my little one' when she wants something. I smiled.

After supper, I called the TV studio. I spoke to one of the assistant producers of the news programme. I gave him our phone number and address. I gave him the number and address of Mr Santini's store as well.

I hope that it was the right thing to do.

# 4

# Mike Murray

*Tuesday*

I went back to work this morning. Mr Santini was very surprised to see me.

'Why aren't you at home in bed? You were really sick yesterday,' he said.

'I'm better now, thank you,' I replied. 'We have a lot of work to do.'

'You're right about that,' Mr Santini said and he laughed.

I worked hard all morning. I put the winter shoes in the shop window. I had nearly finished when I heard a knock on the window.

There was a young man outside in the street. He smiled and waved at me. I didn't look at him. I finished putting the shoes in the window. Then I went back into the store. The young man was waiting for me inside the store.

'You don't remember me,' he said. 'I was at Stanley Park on Sunday afternoon.'

Of course I remembered him. He was the young man who offered me a ride in his car.

'Yes,' I said. 'Now I remember you.'

'Good. I'm one of the assistant producers of the TV news programme, "Voice of Vancouver". My name is Mike Murray. You called the TV studio last night. I was there at the studio when you called.'

*I heard a knock on the window.*

Mr Santini looked at me.

'Is everything all right, Mei?' he asked.

'Yes, yes,' I replied.

Mike Murray introduced himself to Mr Santini.

'My name is Mike Murray. I'm from Vancouver TV. Are you Mr Santini?'

'That's right,' Mr Santini said to him. 'What can I do for you?'

'Well,' Mike Murray said. 'Perhaps you don't know, but this young lady is a very brave person.'

'What do you mean?' Mr Santini asked.

'On Sunday she saved the life of a little boy. The little boy is the son of James Manning, one of the richest, most important men in Vancouver.'

'Is this true, Mei?' Mr Santini asked.

I didn't say anything. I was embarrassed.

'Yes,' Mike Murray went on. 'This young lady jumped into the water. She grabbed the little boy and she swam to the sea wall with him. She saved Tom Manning's life. Then she went away. She didn't say anything.'

'Now I understand,' Mr Santini said. 'Mei was very sick yesterday. But she didn't say anything about the little boy. You're right. She is brave.'

'Tom's parents want to thank Mei,' Mike Murray went on. 'And Mei, if you agree, my TV studio would like to interview you for our news programme.'

'No!' I said. 'I don't want to be on television!'

'Mei,' Mr Santini said. 'This is a great opportunity. Mr Murray can film the interview here in the shop. It will be very good publicity for Santini's Shoe Store.'

'Great!' said Mike Murray. 'Is that OK, Miss Nguyen?'

'Well – I don't know —'

'The answer is "yes",' said Mr Santini.

'Mr Santini!' I said.

'Listen, Mei. You must do this interview. It'll be good for you – and for Santini's Shoe Store.'

Mr Santini turned to Mike. 'When do you want to do the interview?'

'Tomorrow morning,' Mike answered. 'The film crew will be here at ten o'clock.'

Mike Murray left. Mr Santini and I were busy for the rest of the day. But every time a customer came in, Mr Santini said, 'Mei is going to be on TV. She saved the life of James Manning's little boy. You must watch the news programme tomorrow evening.'

When I got home, I told my grandmother. She smiled. She didn't talk about the interview.

'Supper's ready,' she said. 'Let's eat.' Then we watched TV as usual.

Before we went to bed she said, 'Your new blue dress. You must wear your new blue silk dress.'

'Mike Murray has blue eyes,' I thought. 'And he has a nice smile.'

I went to bed early.

# 5

# A Very Exciting Day

*Wednesday*

I got up early this morning. I put on my new blue dress. There was a knock at my bedroom door.

'Come in,' I said.

My grandmother came in. She had a small box in her hand. She gave me the box and I opened it. Inside there was a pair of gold earrings with blue stones.

'These are very special earrings, Mei,' my grandmother said softly.

'They're beautiful!'

'They were a present from your father to your mother,' she said. 'Wear them today.'

I put on the earrings and looked in the mirror. I saw my grandmother's face in the mirror behind me. Did I see tears in her eyes?

'With those earrings and with that blue dress, you are like your mother,' my grandmother said. 'Now come and have breakfast.'

I got to work at 8.30. Mr Santini was already there. Mrs Santini was there too with their two little girls, Barbara and Liliana. Everybody was excited. Mrs Cadish from the flower shop next door brought some yellow roses. I put them in a vase on the counter. Mr Davies from the bakery across the street brought some cakes. Barbara and Liliana ate them all immediately.

Mike Murray arrived at exactly ten o'clock. There were four other people with him. There was a woman. She was going to interview me. And there was a cameraman and two technicians.

Everyone said 'hi' and shook hands. The woman's name was Jane. She was friendly. She asked me some questions and made a note of my answers. Then Tom and his parents arrived and the interview began. At first I was shy and I spoke quietly. Then I began to speak more easily.

This evening I watched the programme on TV with my grandmother. This is how it went.

(First the camera showed Jane standing next to the vase of yellow roses.)

JANE: Good evening. This is Jane Sinclair reporting. This is the story of a brave young woman. This young woman saved the life of a small boy. The small boy's name is Tom Manning. Hello, Tom.

TOM: Hi.

JANE: How old are you, Tom?

TOM: I'm five.

JANE: Can you tell us what you did on Sunday afternoon?

TOM: I went for a walk with my mother along the sea wall in Stanley Park.

JANE: Do you remember what happened?

TOM: I wanted to throw some stones into the water but I fell in.

JANE: What happened next?

TOM: A girl jumped in and saved me. Then I went to the hospital with my Mom.

JANE: Who was the girl who saved you, Tom?

TOM: There she is! She's standing next to you.

(Tom pointed towards me and the camera moved across to me.)

JANE: Ladies and gentlemen, this is Mei Nguyen. She's 18 years old. Mei was born in Hanoi, in Vietnam. She came to Vancouver eight years ago with her grandmother. She works in a shoe store – right here in

Santini's Shoe Store.

(The camera moved around the store and stopped to show the Santini family. They were very pleased and proud. Then the camera moved back to Jane and me.)

JANE: So, Mei – can you tell us about Sunday afternoon? What were you doing in Stanley Park?

ME: I was running. I run every day. My dream is —

JANE: Yes? What is your dream, Mei?

ME: I want to – I want to run in the Olympic Games.

JANE: That's interesting. Do you have a professional trainer?

ME: No. No, I don't.

JANE: Well, good luck. Now, Mei, let's talk some more about Sunday.

ME: I saw Tom. He fell into the water and I jumped in. That's all. Believe me, it was nothing.

(Suddenly Tom ran to me and put his little arms around me.)

TOM'S MOTHER: Mei, you were very brave. You saved our son's life.

(The camera moved over to Tom's parents.)

JANE: And these are Tom's parents, Valerie and James Manning.

MR MANNING: May I say something?

JANE: Please go ahead, Mr Manning.

MR MANNING: I'm a businessman and I believe that money speaks louder than words. Miss Nguyen, I would like to sponsor your training as an athlete. If you say 'yes', we can discuss the details later.

JANE:   That's very generous, Mr Manning. What do you
        say, Mei?
ME:     That's – er – that's very generous of you, sir. But I
        have to speak to my grandmother first.
(The camera then showed us all. Everyone smiled.)
JANE:   Well, ladies and gentlemen. That's all for today
        from Jane Sinclair and 'Voice of Vancouver'.

———

My grandmother turned off the television.

'What does "sponsor" mean?' she asked.

'It means to pay all the costs. Tom's father wants to
pay all the costs for my training. He wants to help me to be
an athlete.'

'Does training cost a lot of money?'

'Yes. A professional trainer is very expensive.'

'And what do you have to do?'

'I have to work hard. I have to win races. That's all.'

Grandmother didn't say anything. For a few minutes we
sat in silence.

Then I asked, 'What do you think, Grandma?'

'Let me think about it, Mei. Let's talk about it in the
morning.'

And we both went to bed.

I lay in my bed in the dark for a long time. I thought
about Mr Manning's offer. I saw myself with an exciting
new life. A life as an athlete. Running and winning.

# 6

## Lunch on Granville Island

*Thursday*

I went into the kitchen. My grandmother was preparing breakfast. She was pale and tired.

'Did you sleep well?' I asked.

'Yes,' she answered. 'But I thought for a long time. I thought about this – this sponsor —'

'Sponsorship,' I said.

'But I also thought a lot about you. I know that you wanted to go to university, my little Mei. You're a clever girl. A job in a shoe store isn't good enough for you. But we need the money.'

'Grandma, please —'

'Don't interrupt me. I also know that you want to be an athlete. But we can't pay for your training. Now you have this offer. But we are very proud, independent people. We have suffered a lot to be free.'

'Yes, I know,' I said.

'If you say "yes", our lives will change. We will not be independent. We will have a debt to this man, this Mr Manning. People with debts are not free.'

I didn't say anything. Perhaps my grandmother was right.

'It's your decision, Mei. I can't stop you if you say "yes". It is a wonderful opportunity. But you must also think about us. This decision will change our lives.'

'I'll think about it, Grandma,' I said. 'But now I have to go to work.'

———

At the store, everyone talked about the news programme and about Mr Manning's offer of sponsorship. I didn't say very much. At 11.30 the telephone rang. Mr Santini answered.

'Santini's Shoe Store, good morning.' Then I heard him say, 'Hold on.'

Mr Santini looked at me. Was the telephone call for me?

'Mei,' said Mr Santini, 'you're wanted on the phone.'

I went to the phone and picked it up.

'Hello?'

'Hello, Mei. This is Mike Murray.'

'Oh, good morning, Mr Murray.'

'Can we have lunch together today? I have to talk to you.'

'Talk to me? What about?'

'Mr Manning asked me to discuss the sponsorship.'

I didn't know what to say.

'What time do you take your lunch break, Mei?'

'At 12.30,' I answered.

'I'll meet you outside the store. OK?'

'Yes, all right. Goodbye,' I said. I put the phone down. Mr Santini was smiling.

'He wants to discuss the sponsorship,' I said.

'But that's wonderful! Mei. Hey, what's the matter? Aren't you happy?'

I wanted to tell Mr Santini about my conversation with my grandmother, but I didn't. I was afraid that I would cry. So I smiled and said, 'I'm OK. I'm a bit tired. Yesterday was a very exciting day.'

'Listen, Mei, I have an idea. Why don't you take the afternoon off? Take a little holiday. Don't come back to work after lunch. Things here in the store are very quiet.'

'Mr Santini, it really isn't necessary. I'm fine —' I tried to say.

'Don't say another word! These are orders from the boss!'

'OK, Mr Santini. That's really kind of you.'

———

At 12.30 Mike Murray was outside the store.

'Hi, Mei,' he said.

'Hello, Mr Murray,' I answered.

'Look, call me Mike, will you? Nobody calls me "Mr Murray"!'

'All right, Mr – sorry – Mike. I'll try.'

'Where do you usually go for lunch?'

'I stay here. I bring a sandwich and an apple. I find a nice, quiet place and I read my book and eat my lunch.'

'Well, today we're going to Granville Island. I know a little restaurant there. It serves very good Vietnamese food.'

'But that's quite far away,' I said.

'We can go on my motorcycle. Do you like riding on motorcycles, Mei?'

'I don't know. I never rode on one.'

'You're not frightened, are you?'

'No,' I said. 'I'm not frightened at all.'

Mike's motorcycle was a big powerful Japanese model. He gave me a helmet. I put it on and got on behind him.

Mike had to drive slowly through the traffic. But when we got on to Granville Bridge he began to go faster.

'OK?' Mike shouted.

'Fine,' I answered. 'It's wonderful!'

When we got to the restaurant, Mike parked the motorcycle and we went inside. Everybody seemed to know him – the manager, the waiters, even some of the other customers. We sat down.

'Are you hungry, Mei?' he asked me.

'Yes! I'm very hungry. And I love Vietnamese food.'

Mike laughed. 'Me too. And this is the best Vietnamese restaurant in Vancouver. What would you like?'

We looked at the menu.

I knew most of the dishes. It wasn't difficult to choose. I chose one of my favourite dishes.

'Would you like something to drink?' Mike asked.

'An orange juice, I guess,' I replied.

Mike ordered our meal. Then he began to talk. 'So, let's talk about the sponsorship.'

There was a vase of blue flowers on the table. I touched their petals. I didn't want to talk about the sponsorship. But I took a deep breath and said, 'I can't accept the offer, Mike.'

'But why not?'

'My grandmother – she doesn't think that it's a good idea.' I put my hands under the table. 'Please – I don't want to talk about it. Can you tell Mr Manning for me? Say "thank you", but I can't accept his offer.'

The waiter brought our food. He put the dishes on the table. 'Enjoy your meal!' he said and went away.

'Let's enjoy our meal, Mei. We don't have to talk about the sponsorship. We can do that some other time. Come on, eat!'

And that's what we did. It was one of the best meals I've ever had. Mike told me all about his family, his job, his life. He made me laugh. I soon forgot my problems. We talked for a long time. Then Mike took me back to the store. I didn't tell him that I had a holiday. Instead I went for a run in Vanier Park.

I didn't tell my grandmother about the lunch and we didn't talk about the sponsorship.

# 7

## A New Friend?

*Friday*

Breakfast was a silent meal this morning. Grandmother and I have to talk about the sponsorship again soon.

At lunch time, I took my sandwich and my book and sat on the steps of the Vancouver Art Gallery. It is the beginning of winter but today it was warm and sunny. There were lots of young people sitting outside. Some sat alone, others were in groups – talking and laughing. I wished that I could be part of one of the groups. I thought about lunch with Mike yesterday. I was another person then – younger and happier.

'But I'm only eighteen!' I thought. 'My life is too quiet, too lonely. I have no friends.'

At that moment, a girl came and sat down beside me on the steps.

*At that moment, a girl came and sat
down beside me on the steps.*

'Did I see you on TV on Wednesday evening?' she asked.

'Yes,' I said. 'That was me.' I looked at her quickly. She was about my age and she had curly red hair and big green eyes.

'Well, you were really brave.'

'Er, thank you,' I said shyly. I didn't know what to say.

'Would you like to come and sit with us?' asked the girl. 'Those are my friends over there. We all work in this area.'

'That would be fun, but I have to get back to work.'

'OK. Another day perhaps,' she said, smiling. She was very friendly. 'By the way, my name's Sandy – Sandy McLaren.'

'I'm pleased to meet you, Sandy. Perhaps I'll see you tomorrow, or on Monday. Goodbye.'

I stood up and walked quickly away. I was angry with myself.

'Mei, why are you so stupid?' I asked myself. 'You were sad because you have no friends. A nice, friendly girl speaks to you. She invites you to sit with her and her friends. And what do you do? You walk away! You are a stupid, stupid girl!'

But then I remembered. 'Maybe I'll meet her again tomorrow,' I thought. 'At lunch time tomorrow, I'll go back to the Art Gallery. I'll sit in the sun and talk to Sandy and her friends. Perhaps they will ask me to go to a movie with them some time. Or invite me to go dancing with them, or to a party.'

When I got back to the store, Mr Santini said, 'There was a phone call for you, Mei. It was that nice young man, Mike Murray.'

'What did he say?' I asked. My cheeks were a little red.

'He'll be here when the store closes. He wants to take you for a coffee. He's a nice young man, Mei. I think he likes you.'

'It's only business, Mr Santini,' I said quickly. 'He wants to talk about the sponsorship.'

'Oh, yes, of course. Only business. I understand, I understand.' He put on his coat and went out to have lunch. He had a big smile on his face.

———

At six o'clock Mike was outside the store. He waved his hand and I went outside.

'Hello, Mei.'

'Hello, Mike.'

'I have only half an hour,' he said. 'I have to be at the television studio by six forty-five. Where can we go for a coffee?'

We went across the road to the Blue Banana Cafe. We sat by a window near the door. People came in and out of the cafe. I looked at them. I tried not to look at Mike. I didn't know what to say. After our coffee arrived, Mike began to speak.

'Er, Mei,' he said. 'I hope you will forgive me. This afternoon I went to speak to your grandmother.'

'What? Why did you do that? How could you —?'

'Mei, take it easy. I'm sorry. James Manning's offer is a

wonderful opportunity for you. You have to accept his sponsorship. Your grandmother has to understand, Mei.'

'What did she say?' I asked.

'It was fine. Your grandmother is a very special person. She loves you very much.'

'I know,' I said. 'And I love her too. But she wants me to live her way.'

'You can't do that, Mei. It's your life. You're young and talented and beautiful.'

'Please, Mike, I have to go home. I have to speak to her.'

'She's all right, believe me. Are you angry with me?'

'No, but —'

'Everything is going to be OK. Finish your coffee, then I'll take you home.'

———

I opened the door of our apartment and called out my grandmother's name.

'I'm in the living room,' she answered.

The television was on. I sat down beside her. I didn't know if she was angry or not.

'Grandmother, I'm sorry. Mike was wrong to come here and upset you.'

'Oh, he didn't upset me. We had a nice long talk.'

'Did you talk about the —?'

'The sponsorship? Yes, we did.'

'And?'

'We'll talk about it on Sunday.'

'On Sunday? Why on Sunday?'

'I invited him to lunch. He likes Vietnamese food. Now,' she said, 'It's time for "Voice of Vancouver". Don't you want to watch it?'

We watched the news programme together. I still don't know if she's angry.

## 8

## Flowers for Mei

*Sunday*

On Saturday, I went back to the steps of the Art Gallery at lunch time. Sandy was there with a friend called Lucy. We started to talk. I wasn't so shy now. Sandy and Lucy work for a travel company. Lucy is going to be married soon. Sandy is studying part-time. She wants to be an actress.

'I'm going to be famous and very, very rich,' she said, laughing. 'I'm going to have beautiful clothes and jewels and a house by a lake.' She pointed to a big, silver car on the other side of the street. 'And I'm going to have a big car with a driver, like that one over there. If you're good, I'll take you all on trips to fabulous places!'

We looked at her and smiled.

'I think that Mei will be famous before you,' said Lucy. 'She's going to run in the Olympic Games!'

It was fun talking to Sandy and Lucy. I almost forgot

the time. I was late when I got back to the store.

'I'm sorry I'm late, Mr Santini,' I said.

'That's all right, Mei,' Mr Santini replied. 'There's a surprise for you. Look behind the counter.'

'What is it?' I asked.

'Why don't you look?'

I went behind the counter and there, on the floor, was an enormous bunch of red roses. There was no card with them.

'But who sent them?' I asked.

'I don't know,' answered Mr Santini.

'So how do you know that they're for me?'

'The man who brought them said, "These are for Miss Mei Nguyen." I guess that they're from that nice young man.'

'But why isn't there a message?' I asked.

'I don't know,' said Mr Santini with a smile. 'Perhaps there is no message. Only the roses. Red roses mean, "I love you", you know! Eighteen beautiful red roses must mean, "I love you very much!" '

'Oh, Mr Santini! It's probably a mistake,' I said. 'The roses are for someone else. The flower shop will probably call this afternoon.'

But the telephone didn't ring, so I took the flowers home.

———

This morning I got up very early and went for a run. Then I came home and helped my grandmother in the kitchen.

At one o'clock, the doorbell rang. Mike was standing

outside. He had a bunch of white flowers in his hand.

'Hello, Mei,' he said. 'These are for you.' He gave me the flowers.

'Come in,' I said. 'Thank you for the flowers. They're lovely.'

My grandmother came into the hall.

'Hello, Mr Murray,' she said. 'It's nice to see you again. More flowers! You are too generous. Mei has never had so many flowers.'

'It's only a little bunch of carnations,' said Mike. He was embarrassed.

'Let's go into the living room,' I said quickly.

We all went into the living room. The vase of red roses was on a small table near the window.

'And what about these?' my grandmother asked. She pointed to the vase.

'They're beautiful roses,' said Mike. 'But I didn't send them to Mei.'

'It was a mistake,' I said. 'They arrived at the shoe store. There was no message with them. Grandma, I didn't say that they were from Mike.'

'I'm sorry, Mei. I thought —' Now my grandmother was embarrassed.

'Don't worry, Mrs Thi,' said Mike with a smile. 'Next time I'll send Mei lots of roses too!'

———

We had lunch. My grandmother had prepared wonderful food. One of the dishes was Cha Ca, a fish dish with lots of spices. It was delicious.

'I didn't send them to Mei.'

'Have some more, Mr Murray,' my grandmother offered.

'I can't,' Mike replied. 'It was fabulous. But I can't eat any more.'

'Then it's time to talk about Mei and her sponsorship,' my grandmother said.

'Good idea,' said Mike.

'I understand now that Mei has to accept it. I understand that she must take this opportunity. She can't work in a shoe store all her life.'

'Oh, Grandma, thank you!' I said.

'You must say thank you to Mike. On Friday, when he came to see me, we talked about debts and about that Mr – Mr —'

'Manning,' said Mike.

'Mr Manning is only paying his debt to you,' Grandmother said. 'You risked your life to save his son. We will have no debt to him, so we are still free. I didn't understand that. I'm sorry that you were unhappy, Mei.'

I stood up. I put my arms around her. 'Oh, Grandma,' I said.

'You're a great lady, Mrs Thi,' Mike said.

'Now Mei will make us some coffee. And Mike will tell us what we have to do next.'

We drank our coffee in the living room. Mike told us about his plans.

'Tomorrow after work, we're going to meet a man called Jack Pearson at the Queen Elizabeth Athletics Club. Jack Pearson is a famous athletics trainer. Mei, you'll have to run at the club. Mr Pearson will watch you run. Then he will decide if he will be your trainer.'

At half past three, Mike had to go. I went to the door with him.

'I like your grandmother,' Mike said.

'She likes you, too,' I answered. 'She's usually quite shy. This is the first time that we've had a guest for lunch.'

'Really?'

'Well, when I was at school, my friends sometimes came to see me. But they never came for a meal. And sometimes my grandmother's Vietnamese friends come to see her.'

'I hope your grandmother will invite me again, Mei,' Mike said. 'Now where did I leave my motorcycle?' He looked across the street.

'There it is,' I said. 'Next to that big silver car.'

'That's strange,' Mike said. 'There's a man in that car. He was in the car when I came.'

I didn't say anything, but I suddenly remembered Sandy. The same car was near the Vancouver Art Gallery yesterday at lunch time.

'Well, Mei, thank you for a lovely lunch.'

'You're very welcome, Mike.'

'See you tomorrow.'

'I'm so nervous about meeting Jack Pearson!' I said with a laugh.

'Don't be nervous. Do your best, that's all.' Mike got on his motorcycle. And he drove off.

I am nervous. In fact I'm very nervous. Tomorrow is an important day in my life.

# 9

## Jack Pearson

*Monday*

I took my track suit and trainers with me to work. All day I thought about meeting Jack Pearson. 'Will he like me?' I thought. 'Will he think that I'm a good runner? What kind of person will he be?'

At six o'clock, Mike was outside the store. The Queen Elizabeth Athletics Club is on Marine Drive. Marine Drive is a very elegant part of the city. We rode very fast on Mike's motorcycle. I love speed. I love the wind on my face. Suddenly, I wasn't nervous.

'I can run as fast as the wind,' I said to myself. 'Jack Pearson will see that I'm a winner!'

Jack was in the entrance to the club.

'Mei,' Mike said, 'this is Jack Pearson. Jack, this is Mei Nguyen. She's going to run for you this evening.'

Jack Pearson shook my hand. 'It's nice to meet you, Mei. Mike and James Manning told me all about you.'

'I'm very happy to meet you, Mr Pearson,' I said.

'Why don't you go and change? The women's changing rooms are over there.' He pointed to a door on the left of the entrance. 'We'll meet you here in ten minutes.'

The changing rooms were warm and bright. There was a good, clean smell of shampoo. I changed quickly into my track suit and trainers. Then I went out to meet Mike and

Jack Pearson. I was ready to run.

———

It was already dark but there were bright lights shining on the track.

'This is like a theatre,' I thought. 'The athletes are like the actors getting ready for a performance.' I went down onto the track. 'This is my world,' I thought. 'This is exactly where I want to be.'

I did some warm-up exercises. Then Jack Pearson came over.

'Go round the track, slowly at first,' he said. 'I want to see how you run. Just relax and take it easy.'

I went round the track.

'Now go round the track again, this time faster,' Jack said. 'Finish with a sprint over the last 50 metres.'

I followed his instructions.

'OK. Now try a 100 metre sprint,' he said. When I had finished, Jack gave me some new instructions. 'This time, run as fast as you can.' He had a stopwatch in his hand. I put my feet in the starting blocks.

'On your marks! Get set! Go!'

I ran the 100 metres and then ran slowly back to Jack Pearson and Mike.

'How was it?' I asked.

'OK. Not bad,' said Jack Pearson. He looked at his stopwatch. '12.06 seconds. I'm sure that you can do better! But not this evening. Go and change. We'll meet you in the club restaurant in half an hour.'

I had a shower and changed into my jeans and sweater.

'Not bad. 12.06 seconds.'

I was tired but happy. I went to the restaurant. Mike and Jack were already there. I sat down at the table.

'Mei, you're a natural runner,' Jack Pearson said. 'And I believe that you can win medals. Perhaps a gold medal. I would like to be your trainer.'

'Thank you, Mr Pearson,' I said.

'Well done, Mei,' said Mike.

'I'm not an easy man,' Jack Pearson said. 'My athletes have to work hard. Are you ready to work hard?'

'Yes,' I answered.

———

We had dinner together at the club restaurant.

'You'll have to train every day,' Jack Pearson said. 'No boy friends. No parties. No holidays. You'll do a morning session before work and an evening session after work. As I said, it won't be easy.'

Mike looked at me. Perhaps he was a little sad.

'So, young lady,' my new trainer said, 'no late nights. In bed by ten o'clock!' He smiled.

'It's already nine-fifteen, Mei,' Mike said. 'I'll have to take you home immediately.'

We all laughed.

'See you tomorrow, Mr Pearson,' I said.

We said good night and Mike took me home.

———

Mike stopped his motorcycle outside the big doors of my apartment building. At that moment, a silver-coloured car drove slowly past us.

'There's your rich neighbour again,' said Mike.

'I don't think that he lives in this street,' I answered. 'People in our street don't have big, expensive cars.'

'Well, perhaps it's a coincidence. But the same car was parked outside the athletics club this evening.'

'I'm sure that it's a coincidence,' I said slowly. But I was worried. I didn't know why.

'Thank you, Mike, for all your kindness,' I said to him.

'It's a pleasure, Mei,' he answered. 'I'll call you soon. Good luck with the training.'

I went into the apartment. My grandmother was in the living room. She always waits for me if I go out in the evening. I told her all about Jack Pearson and what he said to me. But I didn't tell her about the big silver car. Before I went to bed, I looked out of my bedroom window. The silver car was outside the entrance to the building.

## 10

# An Invitation

*Saturday*

The training sessions with Jack Pearson are exhausting! He was right. His athletes have to work very hard! But today is Saturday and I had no session with him.

Sandy invited me to have supper with her family. After work, I took a bus across Burrard Bridge to the university area.

Sandy's father is a history professor at the University of

British Columbia. They live in an old house with a big, beautiful garden. Sandy has three sisters and a brother. They all have red hair and green eyes. Her mother is a sweet woman.

'So you're Mei,' Sandy's mother said. 'Sandy has told us all about you. She says that you live with your grandmother.'

'Yes, that's right,' I answered.

'Next time you come, you must bring her too. We'd like to meet her.'

'That would be nice,' I said. 'I'm sure that she would like to meet you all, too. And you must all come and have lunch with us one day. My grandmother is a wonderful cook.'

Soon it was time for me to go. I said goodbye to Sandy's parents.

'Sandy, why don't you drive Mei home?' said her father. 'You can take my car. The keys are in the hall.'

'That's very kind of you, Mr McLaren,' I said. 'But I can take the bus. It's not late —'

'Nonsense! Sandy loves to use my car,' he said with a laugh.

'Thanks, Dad,' said Sandy. She gave him a kiss on the cheek.

'Goodbye, Mei,' Sandy's mother said. 'Come again soon.'

'Thank you, Mrs McLaren. And thank you for everything. You have a lovely family. Sandy is very lucky! I would love to have brothers and sisters.'

'They're not always so good!' Sandy laughed. 'They were good this evening, because you were there. Sometimes I wish that I didn't have brothers and sisters!'

We got into the car and drove off. We turned onto the main road. I looked back. I wanted to wave 'goodbye'. Sandy's mother wasn't there.

And then I saw the big silver car.

I didn't say anything to Sandy. 'That car is following me,' I thought. Now I was scared.

Sandy turned on the radio. We listened to the music in silence for a few minutes. Then she said, 'What's wrong, Mei?'

'Nothing,' I said. 'Why?'

'You're very quiet. Are you worried about my driving?'

'Oh, no, of course not! You drive very well.'

'Then what is it?'

'There's a car behind us.'

Sandy looked in the mirror. 'The silver one?' she asked.

'Yes,' I replied. 'It's always following me. Everywhere that I go. It's in the street where I live. At the Queen Elizabeth Club. The man in that car is following me. Sandy, I'm scared.'

'Are you sure?' asked Sandy.

'I wasn't sure until now. Now I know.'

'But who is he? What does he want?'

'I don't know, Sandy. I don't know.'

'Has the driver spoken to you?'

'No. He just follows me in his car.'

'Have you seen his face?' she asked.

'The man in that car is following me.'

'No, never. I usually see the car in the evening when it's too dark.'

'So you've never seen the driver during the day?'

'Well, yes,' I said. 'Once. It was the first day that I met you and Lucy outside the Art Gallery.'

'Yes, I remember! Did he follow you then?'

'I don't know. Maybe,' I replied. 'Sandy, what am I going to do? I'm scared. I don't like it!'

'You could go to the police. But he hasn't hurt you. He hasn't even spoken to you.'

'I – I think that he sent me roses,' I said. 'Eighteen red roses arrived at the store. There was no card with them.'

Sandy thought for a few moments. Then she said, 'Mei, I don't think that this man wants to hurt you. Wait a little while. Perhaps, when you are ready, confront him.'

'Confront him? You mean – speak to him?'

'Yes. Walk up to the car and knock on the window. Ask him what he wants.'

'Perhaps you're right,' I said. 'I have to think about it.'

Sandy left me outside my apartment building. The car wasn't in the street. She is right. That man has no reason to hurt me. But I don't like it. I don't like it at all.

It is my grandmother's birthday tomorrow. Mike has invited us out to a restaurant for brunch – a very early lunch. Perhaps I can ask him what to do.

# 11

# The Man in the Silver Car

*Sunday*

Today was an amazing day. I cannot believe the things that happened. I want to think about them all. And I want to write them down, one at a time.

When I got up, I made some tea. My grandmother was still in bed, so I took her a cup.

'Happy birthday, Grandma!' I said. I gave her a present. 'This is for you with lots of love.'

She opened the parcel.

'A lovely, warm scarf!' she said. 'And it's green. My favourite colour.'

'Wear it when you come to see me run,' I said. 'I want you to be there. I want you to meet Jack Pearson. And I want Jack Pearson to meet you. I'm so proud of you, Grandma.'

'Thank you, my darling Mei. I'll wear it today when we go out.' I put the scarf around her shoulders.

'And can I wear the special earrings again? Please, Grandma, please?'

'Of course you can. But first, tell me something. What is this "brunch"?'

'Well, it's not breakfast and it's not lunch. It's something between the two. We can't have a big meal because I'm training this afternoon.'

'But what will they give us to eat?'

'Delicious things, Grandma. I promise. Now let's get ready.'

——

When Mike arrived at eleven o'clock, we were both ready to go out. Mike looked at us both and said, 'Two beautiful women! A beautiful sunny day! What more can a man want?' My grandmother was very pleased and excited.

We stood for a moment at the entrance to our building. It was a beautiful, sunny morning. It was cold but the sky was clear and very blue. There were some children playing in the street. I was happy to be alive.

Then I saw the silver car. It was on the other side of the street.

I thought of Sandy and I decided. Now was the moment to confront the man.

'Wait a minute,' I said to Mike and my grandmother.

I crossed the street quickly and knocked on the driver's window. My hand shook. I was afraid but I was angry, too. The man in the car put his hands over his face for a few seconds. Then he opened the door and got out of the car. He was a short man, aged about fifty. He was Vietnamese.

'What do you want?' I shouted in Vietnamese. 'Why do you follow me?'

He looked at me. He didn't say a word. Then he said my name. 'Mei?'

Mike and my grandmother walked towards the car. They stood behind me.

'Is everything all right, Mei?' Mike asked.

My grandmother came and stood beside me. She and

*Then he opened the door and got out of the car.*

the man looked at each other.

There was a long silence.

'No!' my grandmother said softly in Vietnamese. 'It's impossible! I don't believe it!'

'Yes, Lan Thi,' said the man. 'It's true.'

My grandmother's face was wet with tears.

She put her arms around the man.

He touched my grandmother's face. He touched her tears. He said her name again and again.

Then my grandmother turned to me.

'Mei,' she said. 'This is your father, Loi.'

'My father?' I said. 'But my father is dead. You're not my father! My father was wounded in the war. He died.'

'No, Mei. I am your father,' said the man. 'I didn't die. I was badly wounded, but I didn't die.'

I didn't know what to say. I began to cry.

'Perhaps this is not the place to have this conversation,' Mike said. 'Let's go back to the apartment.'

'You're right,' my grandmother said.

Her face was happy and beautiful. 'Come, Loi,' she said. 'Come up to our apartment. Come and tell us how you found us! Tell us everything.'

My grandmother held the man's arm and they crossed the street.

'This isn't a good time for me to be here,' said Mike. 'We can have brunch another day.'

'Mike,' I said. 'Mike, this is all very strange —'

'It's not strange, Mei. It's wonderful. Be happy. Now go with your father and grandma. Call me this evening.'

———

We went up into our apartment. The man – Loi – my father – took off his coat and gave it to me. It was a soft, expensive coat. I put it with our old, cheap coats in the hall. I stood and I looked at the coats. I didn't want to go and talk to him.

'Why am I not happy?' I asked myself. I didn't understand.

'Mei!' my grandmother called. 'What are you doing? We're in the kitchen!'

I went into the kitchen. My grandmother made green tea.

'Come sit beside me, Mei,' my father said. I sat down. He put out his hand and touched my earrings. 'I gave these earrings to your mother on our wedding day – the day that we married,' he said. 'These earrings helped me to find you.'

'I don't understand,' I said. My voice was cold. I didn't want to look at him.

'Mei,' said my grandmother. 'What's the matter with you?'

'It's all right, Lan,' said my father. 'It's a terrible shock for Mei. I understand. It was a shock for me too.'

'If you're my father,' I said angrily, 'where have you been all these years? It's too late. We don't want you in our lives.'

'Mei!' my grandmother said. 'What are you saying?'

'I understand her,' my father said. 'I will tell you my story. Then you can decide. You can decide if you want me in your life or not.'

# 12

## Loi's Story

'Until about two weeks ago,' said Loi, 'I was a man with no past. My new life began in the summer of 1979. My new life began on a very small, very poor farm near the border of Cambodia and Laos. The farmer's children found me in the forest. I had a serious head wound. I was dying.

'When I woke up in the farmer's house, I didn't know my name. My memory had gone. I didn't remember anything. I spoke Vietnamese but the farmer only spoke a few words of Vietnamese. I had no identity papers. I only had a photograph. It was a photograph of a young woman. She was wearing gold earrings with blue stones. But I didn't remember her. Was she my fiancée? My sister? My wife? I didn't know.

'I stayed with the family for two months. When I was better, I left them. They gave me some clothes and a little food. I walked during the night. I slept in the forest during the day. I wanted to get to the Vietnam border but I had no map. The farmer told me that I must go south-east.

'I walked for almost two weeks. I often saw Cambodian soldiers and jeeps. But they didn't see me. Then one day I heard people speaking our language. They were people going to work in the fields. I knew then that I was back in my country. I was safe. I was safe but I had no place to go. I didn't know what to do.

'I went to Hanoi. I walked in the streets of the city.

'Until about two weeks ago, I was a man with no past.'

"Maybe I'll see someone who knows me. Maybe someone will say my name," I thought. But no one knew me. Then I found that I could speak English and French. It's strange, isn't it? You can forget your name, but not the languages that you know.

'I got a job as an interpreter. When I had some money, I paid a man to make me some identity papers. My new name was Nhu Quang. It's my name now.

'Very slowly I made a new life. But it wasn't a real life. I had no family, no friends. I met some Canadian people in my work. I decided then to leave Vietnam. I came to Canada ten years ago. I was lucky. I began to work with computers. I studied computer programming. I began to write my own programmes. I invented a computer game. It was very popular. I made a lot of money. I'm a rich man now.

'I'm married. I have a new family. My wife is Canadian. We have two little boys. They are your brothers, Mei. For ten years I have lived only in the present.

'Then one evening, I was watching a news programme on TV. I saw a young Vietnamese girl. She had saved a small boy. I couldn't believe it! She was the girl in the photograph. She had the same gold earrings with blue stones. Her name was Mei Nguyen.

'I didn't know what to do. I spoke to my wife. I showed her the old photograph – yes, I still have it.

' "Quang," my wife said, "you must find this girl. This is your chance. Perhaps it's a coincidence. Perhaps it's not. You will never be happy if you don't find her."

'It was easy to find you. The interview was in Santini's Shoe Store.

'Slowly, my memory came back. I remembered my mother and father, my first wife, Le Ly. I remembered our wedding, our baby girl, Mei. I remembered the war. But I couldn't decide what to do. I wanted to be with you, Mei. I wanted to be part of your lives. But I didn't know if you would want me.

'I sent Mei some roses,' Loi said to Grandma. 'I followed her. I watched her. Today she spoke to me. She was angry with me. She's still angry with me. But I hope now that she will understand me.'

———

My father finished his story. My grandmother had tears in her eyes.

'I'm sorry,' I said. 'I need a little time to think.'

'Of course,' my father replied. 'I understand.'

'Mei has to be at her training session at three o'clock,' said my grandmother. 'We have to have some lunch – I mean brunch.'

My father laughed. 'It's too late for brunch, Lan Thi,' he said. 'Let's have a snack. Then I'll drive Mei to her training session.'

'I want to go to the training session, too,' my grandmother said. 'And I'm going to wear my birthday present, my new green scarf!'

———

When I woke up this morning, I was a person with one kind of life. This evening, I am a person with another, very different life. My grandmother and I are not alone in the world now. We are part of a family. Tomorrow we are going to meet my father's Canadian wife and their two little boys – my brothers.

My mother said to me before she died, 'Mei, live your life fully. Be happy! Be brave! Be successful!' I am happy to have my father and my new Canadian family. People say that I was brave when I saved the little boy. Perhaps soon I'll be successful. I'll do everything that I can to win an Olympic Gold Medal. Then perhaps my mother's wishes and my dream will come true.

# Points for Understanding

1 What is Mei's dream?
2 Who does Mei live with? Why?
3 Which country did Mei come from?
4 What did Mei's mother say to Mei?

1 What happened to the little boy?
2 What did Mei do?
3 Why didn't Mei want to tell her grandmother what happened?
4 'My grandmother notices everything.' What did Mei's grandmother notice?
5 What did Mei's grandmother say then?

1 Did Mei take any medicine the next morning?
2 What did Mr Santini ask Mei?
3 What did Mr Santini tell Mei to do?
4 How did Mei know that she was better?
5 Who did Mei see on TV?
6 What did the woman ask Mei to do?
7 Did Mei want to do anything?
8 What did Mei's grandmother want Mei to do?

1 Who came to Santini's Shoe Store?
2 What did the TV studio want to do?
3 What did Mr Santini say to Mei?
4 What did Mr Santini say to his customers?
5 What did Mei's grandmother want Mei to wear?

1  What was in the box that Mei's grandmother gave to Mei?
2  What was Jane Sinclair going to do?
3  What did Mr Manning say to Mei?
4  What did Mei reply?
5  What costs a lot of money?
6  Was Mei excited? What did she think about that night?

6

1  Why did Mei's grandmother say, 'We won't be independent'?
2  Why did Mike Murray want to talk to Mei?
3  Where did Mike Murray take Mei?
4  What did Mei say to Mike about the sponsorship?
5  What did Mike reply?

7

1  What did the young woman first ask Mei?
2  What did she invite Mei to do then?
3  What did Mei reply?
4  Why was Mei angry with herself?
5  Who had Mike spoken to?
6  Was Mei pleased?
7  Was Mei's grandmother angry?

8

1  Was Mei shy when she met Sandy and Lucy?
2  What was the surprise for Mei at Santini's Shoe Store?
3  What did Mike bring?
4  Why was Mike embarrassed?
5  Why was Mei's grandmother embarrassed?
6  Why did Mei's grandmother say, 'We will have no debt to him'?
7  What may Jack Pearson do?

1 Was Mei nervous when she arrived at the athletics club?
2 What did Jack Pearson tell Mei to do first?
3 Why is an athletics track like a theatre?
4 How many times did Mei run a 100 metre sprint?
5 How do Jack Pearson's athletes have to work?
6 What was outside the entrance to the apartment building?

## 10

1 Where did Mei go for supper?
2 What is always following Mei?
3 What did Sandy tell Mei to do?

## 11

1 Who does Mei want her grandmother to meet?
2 What did Mei decide to do when she saw the silver car?
3 What did Mei's grandmother say when she saw the man?
4 What helped Loi to find Mei?
5 Was Mei pleased at first?

## 12

1 What did Loi remember when he woke up in the farmer's house?
2 What was the only thing he had?
3 How did he get a new name?
4 How did Loi become rich?

Published by Macmillan Heinemann ELT
Between Towns Road, Oxford OX4 3PP
Macmillan Heinemann ELT is an imprint of
Macmillan Publishers Limited
Companies and representatives throughout the world

ISBN 0 435 27309 4

First published 1999
Design and illustration © Macmillan Publishers Limited 2002
Heinemann is a registered trademark of Reed Educational and Professional Publishing Limited
This version first published 2002

For Candice

Designed by Sue Vaudin
Illustrated by Beryl Saunders, Map on page 4 by John Gilkes
Cover by Arlene Adams and Marketplace Design

Printed in China

2006 2005 2004 2003 2002
10   9   8   7   6   5   4   3   2